VAMPIRE FAYE ACADEMY

BOOK 1

VALOUR AND HOPE

LEON LOWE

AuthorHouse™
1663 Liberty Drive
Bloomington, IN 47403
www.authorhouse.com
Phone: 833-262-8899

Because of the dynamic nature of the Internet, any web addresses or links contained in this book may have changed since publication and may no longer be valid. The views expressed in this work are solely those of the author and do not necessarily reflect the views of the publisher, and the publisher hereby disclaims any responsibility for them.

Any people depicted in stock imagery provided by Getty Images are models, and such images are being used for illustrative purposes only. Certain stock imagery © Getty Images.

This book is printed on acid-free paper.

ISBN: 978-1-7283-7980-7 (sc)
ISBN: 978-1-7283-7981-4 (e)

Library of Congress Control Number: 2022924122

Print information available on the last page.

Published by AuthorHouse 02/13/2023

authorHOUSE®

CONTENTS

1
CHAPTER

ANCIENT DREAM

Terence Valour is a dark-skinned man in his mid-twenties. He has cocoa skin and is medium tall. He lives his work. He is a martial arts instructor, personal trainer, nutritionist and cafe owner. Terence Valour lives on top of his gym and restaurant in a three-story maisonette. He runs specialist nutrition pharmacies in the daytime and works at his cafe. He is a martial arts instructor at night. Terence Valour is a hardworking, earnest, principled nutritionist, cook, and dedicated fitness instructor. It's night, and it's been a hard day's work at the cafe.

The fitness classes are once a fortnight to spare Terrence the burden of burnout. He has a three-day working week as a nutritionist in his ground-level holistic spa gymnasium. Still, he does the cooking seven days a week.

On this particular day, he receives news of a loved one. A letter is posted through his door telling him his great-grandfather has passed away. He must attend his funeral in one month in Maidstone, as he may stand to inherit seven per cent of his great fortune. He goes about his day as usual, and soon the night settles in, and he goes into his bedroom for a night's sleep.

Terrence experiences rapid eye movement in his sleep. He falls into a dream that seems not only vivid but authentic and natural to the touch.

In the real world, there is natural lighting. Terrence's eyes open, waking up in a dream reality where everything seems normal. However, the scene is more of a dreamlike state in a bluish-white haze of an atmosphere.

He wakes mystified and what appears, smells, feels, tastes, looks and haunts as the real world, but when Terrence opens his eyes, he walks out of bed and walks towards the window. Although it may all seem completely real, Terrence now appears to be in a dream or a dream world.

He wakes up and sets his body forward in a quickened huff and pace. He arises from the bed and then suddenly snaps back to his senses, slowly walking towards what appears to be an opening and closing window.

The window opens and shuts to its independent valuation. The window closes several times until the window stays open and gently blows.

The partially see-through light white curtains remain in the air whilst the wind blows into the room freely.

Then he hears the soft voice of a lady singing. The voice tells him," Terrence, it's me, your guardian angel.

Do not be afraid to come from behind that window and explore the realm of your ancestors". A calmly exuberant Terrence listens with awe and excitement whilst walking with a soft and understanding tone and says to the ancient. "yes, coming great mother,",,

Terrence hurries and climbs out of the window. He safely lands on the ground, but when he looks around, he is in what appears to be a temple with many ancient statues.

Terrence walks along and looks at the temple in its splendour: twelve figures on one side and twelve on the other.

The great mother speaks again, "look long and hard, destined warrior. They are the statutes and images of your most ancient and legendary ancestors, even your great-grandfather, who has recently come to join us.

He also is attributed to this hall, and soon you shall also be".

He stops and looks at the sixth statue on the right and beholds its image.

The figure suddenly stops and turns to him.

The statue pops from the two altars and stands in front of Terrence.

The figure says, "I am your ancient father of times not long ago.

I am trey Lorenzo, your great-grandfather from the Englands industrial era.

Fith earl of kent and skilled warrior in the art of kickboxing".

An astonished and enamoured Terrance asks an essential question in a voice of stillness and quiet zeal. He asks, "what am I doing here, why am I here, and what do my ancestors want from me"?

The ancient warrior, with a tremendous upright posture, tells him. "A great trial is coming upon you soon.

All your relatives are ancient warriors. Due to this, it is only fitting that we heed our beloved child. Great trials lay ahead".

The great mother intervenes and, with quiet urgency, tells him.

"A great evil is being unleashed. Realms are colliding spirit forces are clashing to stop this evil from entering the living world. Still, storm shows the great evil has all the forces of good and is now in the realm of the living, waiting to be completely submerged and immersed in the land of the living".

Terrence, with a sympathetic tone, asks gently. "So what do you want with me"?

The Edwardian ancient statute tells Terrence.

"We believe that with you ascending from great warriors. You are the only one that can stop this great evil from taking over the earth and grinding the dreams of the good into ash and rubble."

. Suddenly a flame of fire is thrown across the hall. The ancient statute screams and yelps as he turns to do battle.

Suddenly, in a powerful, awe-inspiring tone, the great mother tells Terrence. "My son of warriors, this is over"!

Terrence awakes back in his bed from his dream. He sets up in a lustrous sweat and pants heavily and expletively to himself, "who,w what was that"?

2
CHAPTER

FREEDOM HOTEL

Grace attends college as a fashion tutor. Grace is twenty-five and is white with Asian features.

When she is not tutoring at the college, she is at the fashion house working on the next project with her models, maids and fashion masters.

The fashion house is a fantastic countryside mansion and individual workhouse which fuels a seemingly large business.

Grace Hope is a vibrant, dedicated hard worker who lives in a workhouse mansion with her sisters and cousins. On this workhouse mansion, there is also a plot of land owned by Grace Hope and her family.

In graces spear time, when she is not working on fashion projects, she tends to the chicken and dairy cows on the farm.

One day the house gets a government inspection, and as head of the house, the inspector sees Grace.

The inspector inspects and, in the end, decides to comment on the house, saying that he has only seen females and that there are not enough males.

Grace tells him they are family, and if the male side of the family came to stay, they would feel out of place "if they came to stay".

The government inspector sees no powerful men. He leaves the ladies alone, promising to return another day to give them a workhouse rating.

Grace agrees and expects a regeneration grant to get new equipment. One month passes; the only difference is that her cousins have gone missing. Tom, the governor inspectorate, arrives again, and grace asks, "where are my cousins"? Tom, the cruel governor, simply tells her they have been selected to work at another house. Grace explains that it is not how things are done and that they are in their natural home around family members. Tom soon drugs and takes Grace away, and she finds that she awakes in another bedroom with an empty bottle and a syringe beside her. She had been drugged and made to drink alcohol. Tom walks up to her and says did you enjoy your sleep. Grace mumbles, "I don't know where I am. Please tell me where we are"? Tom walks away, and Grace falls asleep again.

Grace lays in the middle of a bed in pain. She looks around and then sees an open window. Grace jumps out of the window and runs away.

She looks at a signpost and realises she is four tens away from her village retreat. She hitchhikes back to her home and finds it has been cleared out and sold.

When she checks the date, she finds that she has been gone for six months. When grace leaves, she meets with tom, and he tells her she should not be there.

She responds by telling him she escaped through a window. He tells her the rooms do not have windows. He grabs her, and cuffs appear in her hand. She then cuffs him to the stairway. She leaves the house and makes her escape with his keys.

Grace takes toms car to a police station and reports how her life has been for the last six months.

The police officer she speaks to seems sympathetic and then arrests her.

Grace seeks help from the police but does not find it. The policemen that she talked to lock her away in a jail cell, and she has to find a way to escape from her jail cell.

Again a pair of magic keys appear in her hand.

She says to herself, "where on earth did I get these powers" just then, a fairy appears to her and says, "not on earth but from the spirit realm.

I am your guardian fairy Espanya here to guard, protect and grant you natural magic".

A confused Grace Hope looks at her fairy with great awe, surprise and suspicion. "So you are my fairy, why me? Why have I got a fairy". The fairy says, "well, that is because you are a fairy as well. All will become clear first. We will have to get you out of here". Grace uses the key to burst out of the jail cell. On her way out of the police station, she comes across twelve violent officers. The fairy tells her. "This is where you learn to use battle magic. Hope, remember you have the magic of the Faye people. Call on it"! "How"! "Faye people use vibration energies to access their magic. We vibrate with the frequency of nature". In a deep, bold voice, she looks around and says to the fairy, although the corrupted police officers think she is talking about them. "And how do I do that"? The arresting officer turns and says. "Who are you talking to? Are you sure it is us"? A second corrupt police officer responds with. "Turn round and go back to your cell. That's how you do that". On turning and slightly shifting, almost agreeably, Grace gets a new notion. "No"! The second officer sees her revolution and asks rudely.

"Are you getting brave all of a sudden, do as you are told". Grace begins to fill the power of nature around her, and soon a graceful wind begins to swoosh around her. She appears overcome with emotion. All the sorrow, grief and despair start to crush around her. Her power level continues to increase, and she says to them before exacting swift vengeance. "I see it now. My power comes from within, all the years working on the form, the tendency to care for people's graceful image. There are things I hold sacred, and your corrupt laws are not one of them. Today the pimps, corruptors, thieves and scoundrels have lost the battle. By the winds of the hollow earth, I summon a whirlwind; come forth". Suddenly the air slowly becomes dense.

Heavy wind palpitations engulf the area, and a quick rush of air is felt through the jail corridor.

The twelve corrupt police officials are blown away and rendered unconscious. Grace approaches them with a restless assurance about her. She walks up to them whilst they are on the floor and retrieves the keys to the police station. A voice from across the jail calls out to her. "Excuse me, Faye person, can you help me please"? In one of the cells is an old oriental man lying chained to the walls. She calls back to him. "Who are you, and how do I know I can trust you"? The tattered-haired elderly and the infirmed man tells her. "I am protege. I am a political prisoner.

I was condemned to this cell by powerful forces beyond your known government. Release me from these chains. I will tell you all you need to know"!

A bemused and bewildered Grace asks with a tone of insecurity.

"How do I know I can trust you"? Protege simply tells her. " you can trust me, Grace.

I am the one who sent you the fairy to guard and protect you and show you the world.

Let me out of here, and I will take you to my hotel.

This hotel is a blissful sanctuary where my wife and I cook for the homeless in need and people who are wary. When we got behind on one of our bills, the sheriff took us into his custody and tricked me into these cuffs".

Grace readied the keys and opened the door. She slowly approaches the entry saying, "I'm coming in now", but when she gets there, it seems empty inside. Just then, a strange flash of lightning evades the door, and a great age-old oriental man stands at the exit in apparel he had seemed fit, healthy and strong for someone of old age.

In a content yet boastful expression, the man stands there and says. "The great Wizard and Watcher of the sacred warriors are finally free. Come with me, Hope".

They leave the station and arrive at the sanctuary hotel.

The hotel is large and winding with magnificent splendour.

The walls are gold with a luxury cream border.

The carpets are grey when you feel or touch them; they have a soft Wooley type of texture that makes you want to take off your shoes and walk barefoot.

Inside, the luxury hotel contains around 200 apartment-type suites for paying guests and the rest for guests who require charity and a little bit of tender loving care.

Protege shows Hope around. He shows her the dining room, which can accommodate up to 500 guests.

The dining room appears to be a place of splendour. With golden vases, cream curtains, and red crushed soft and luxurious cushioned furnishings, all made from firm memory foam. The hall is walled with green marble and pine flooring. Everything about it screams luxury.

Protege then shows hope in and around the conference rooms as he explains to her. "We have twelve conference rooms on each level of this six-story hotel, that's seventy-two conference rooms used for business meetings and educational experiences.

Each of our conference rooms is sixty square meters. They have a small kitchen, a bathroom and plenty of workshop apparatus for different industrious use.

Hotel management is based on education and business, which resulted in industry. Active pursuits had been a vital topic for the hotel staff and hosts. When Protege finished in the conference room, he toured hope around the basement spas.

"In this basement are 200 individual spa rooms with private sleeping quarters, each with a kitchen diner and on-call room service.

The sleeping quarters are twenty square meters, and the spa area is forty square meters. Every room upstairs has this quality also, but in the basement, there is a collection of swimming pools, hydrotherapy pools, jacuzzi tubs and spa showers.

If you want the spa experience, booking some time on the lower levels would be best. Protege shows Hope around the basement and then the ground and first level.

Hope is amazed by the splendour of the hotel.

She turns to Protege and says, "this place is glorious. How long did it take you to get a place like this"? Protege tells her.

I worked hard for ten years, and soon I had two levels of a quarter-acre hotel. We would add another level and give it individualism every two years.

The basement is a wellness spa. The ground level is designed for catering, dining, comfort, check-in and lounging.

The first level is designed to hold arcades, games, and sports.

The second level is designed as a cinema and movie dome with eateries.

The third level is designed to accommodate library books for education and a computer study bay for entertainment and mental pursuits.

The fourth level is designated to massage therapy and gymnasium training. The final two levels are solely accommodation suites for sleeping, eating and washing.

Now let us take you to your suite. We will talk more about your arrangements in the morning".

A suspicious Grace, with a nervous tremble and hyper-ventilating breath, asks Protege, "am I safe here".

Protege responds, "I assure you, You are entirely comfortable here in this hotel with my wife and me. The people after you don't like me because of my work at the sanctuary. Grace, they were devils, not me. If you want, I can teach you Martial arts. My friend Terrence is a martial arts trainer, and he visits once a month to tutor us and lend us nutrition.

He is our doctor. I will get him to take a look at you when he arrives in the morning".

Grace is shown to her luxury space room of one hundred and twenty square meters and slowly enters, saying to protege.

"Thank you, Protege, for all of your help" Grace walks into her hotel suite, and Protege tells her. "I'll have someone bring you up some lovely food and drink. What would you like"? Grace lays down and tells him, "anything, as long as it is Halal". Protege responds, "I will bring you a chicken curry and a bottle of fizzy pop. We make the slow-cooked stuff here. I'll have it with you in twenty minutes." Protege leaves for the kitchen. Grace sits in her one hundred and twenty square meter luxury suite. She looks around at its opulent and expensive interiors and space. Grace soon gets restless and decides to look around the hotel. She takes a picture on her phone of the level she's on and then takes the elevator to the top floor. The elevator door opens onto a foyer reception area with a hall leading into a dining room area. This then leads to four rooms opposite each other two are for storing food, two are for cooking food, and three are for food preparation. The last door is locked. As she tries to unlock it, banging comes from the room. Grace gets creeped out and runs back to her suite. She sneaks in and then lays on her bed with an ephemeral tactile charm. Protege enters the room with her food, not admittedly not noticing her heavy breathing and nervous tone, putting the food on her table opposite her and saying. "Enjoy your meal, and feel free to look around the hotel but do not go where the doors are locked". Protege exits the room. Grace sits up to eat her meal. The night closes in, and the hotel seems asleep. Grace listens to the advice of Protege and goes for a walk. She goes back to the place where she saw the thumping locked door. She attempts to open it and hears the words "you may enter" when she does. Grace walks through the room and opens another door which leads into a hall. Stepping into the arena, she comes across thirty winged students sitting around a dinner table feasting. The hotel she is in doubles as a Faye magic university. The senior tutor, a lady named Faye with an excellent grey wingspan, says to grace. "Come along, young Faye and welcome to your new residence halls". "What is this place," asks Grace. Lenora, the principal tutor, tells her. "This is the magic university for Faye, and you have been specially selected as a student". "Student, a student of what"? Asks agrace, principal tutor Lenora explains, "a student of magic since your 21st birthday, you have been chosen as a member of noble Faye blood to join this academy". A bemused and wondrous grace looks around at all the students and then says. "I'm nobility", Lenora explains to grace. "Your mother is the sister of the Faye queen, and your father is a close cousin. Both of them enjoy a high level of nobility". A still nervous and afraid Grace asks, " why was I kidnapped? Is it because of my nobility" Lenora tells her with a stern yet caring expression. "Well, not exactly. Meet me later, and I will tell you all you need to know. There are things we cannot discuss publicly". Grace asks, "What type of lessons do we learn here"? Lenora tells her. " We study five types of magic in academia: crystal, truth chant, protection, healing, and conjuring magic. We also hold classes on practical, technical and theoretical artisan creativity. This hotel Academy also endows itself with the magical qualities of etiquette. In fact, the name of this hotel is the magic hotel academy of etiquette.

Welcome to the Academy ranks". With an open-mouthed, bemused look, Grace asks. "Why have I only been selected now"?

Lenora's face sinks, and she sighs, telling Grace. " I thought you would ask that. This academy is solely for Faye and Vampire. This academy, in particular, is for royal Faye and Vampyre. Faye and Vampyre have existed in close harmony for thousands of millennia. We are both woodland creatures. We are natural shape-shifters and can make our basic winged forms visible or shape-shifting into a normal human". Grace, with an almost surprised look, says to her.

And you are a Vampyre"? Lenora tells her. I am a cross between a grand Vampyre and a high-level nymph.

Grace gazes up at Lenora. She appreciates her majesty and her wingspan. "Am I a Faye"? Lenora, in a tone of subtleness, tells her.

"Yes, indeed, you are a Faye." Young adult Grace seems meek and timid as she slowly whispers as if in the presence of a loving family.

"What happens now? When will I see my cousins?". The sound and graceful Lenora tells her. "We will send out a search party soon enough, but for now, get some rest, eat and read up on our academy practices".

Grace attends the dinner, eats up and goes back to her room. She reads up on the academy's practices and rules.

She comes across an article that tells a story of a small-town young adult named Terrence Valour and how he is a fitness instructor, a cook and a medical nutritionist.

The article shows how he taught many women to kickbox in the local area where grace is only fifteen miles away.

Grace goes exploring in hopes of finding her tutor, who is also the same age. She leaves the academy on her motorbike and drives down the lane.

On the way to Terrence's mini tower and business, she gets followed by what appears to be a government agent.

The agent drives behind her motorcycle, and when she realises, she speeds up, but the driver behind pursues.

She speeds away quickly, weening through traffic and just narrowly missing oncoming vehicles. The driver followers her until she arrives at Terrence Valours restaurant and gymnasium.

She runs to the door and screams, "Help me. I am being chased". Terrence is sleeping on third floor when Terrence wakes from the noise.

He looks outside his window and sees a tall man in a business suit grasping at a young lady who seems partially dressed, although in designer clothes.

She decides she will seek him out to help her find her cousins.

3

TEACHERS TRAINING

Terrence fights off the pimp, and the pimp puts up a battle but is far from a match for Terrence. The pimp warns Terrence.

"Give over the Faye", Terrence responds!

"why I ain't afraid of you,"

The pimp, with a warlock expression of anger, says, "I don't know why you are a match for me, but you have begun to deal in forces you can barely imagine. I'll get you back for this"!

The pimp drives off, and Terrence and Grace enter Terrence's building and settle into the cafe. Terrence collects his meal, and they begin to speak with each other.

Grace eats an oiled honey vinaigrette-dressed chicken salad with Terrence. She says, after swallowing food. "You choose to protect me from the evil man like I knew you would. A straight edge Terrence responds to Grace's conversation with, "Do you know me?

"Sorry, my name is Grace Hope, Student and Patreon of the academy of magic. Pleased to meet you. I read your file and decided to investigate".

"Or maybe you had seen a few online interviews of me and decided you needed my help. What kind of trouble are you in"? Some evil demons are after me, and I need help from magical folk like you". "I am not at full maturity for another three days. Although I know how to battle against magic using martial arts, I have not unlocked my potential as a vampire. How about you"? "I reached full maturity as a Faye princess a few days ago. I was even told that I am on the same level as you are". "In two days, I will be the last full-blood vampire prince on earth. I guess you are saying that without your first cousins and sisters, the same could be said for you". "that is precisely what it is. We need to bring down this evil coven immediately, and I know you can do it. Please help me. "That is all well and true. For all intents and purposes, you have my help and unconditional affection. Still, before we go any further, I start my new career at the academy today. We will do it, but we must run it past higher management. We might even get professional and quality support". Grace and Terrence leave the building and set off in Terrence's car on the way to the academy. At the academy. Principal protege, vice principal Lenora and Protege's wife Carrelli, the potion mistress. Spencer, the shaman. Olive, the practical spells teacher and jun, the alchemy and elements specialist, are all in the underground basement meeting room. The room is wide and spacious, with a library and conference office, a dining area, and a cafeteria. All the seats appear comfortable and soft. The colours in the room are red and oak brown with golden ornaments. One of the golden ornaments was of a dragon, and it stood at six feet tall the other was of a winged fairy and stood roughly the same size as the dragon. The principal protege tells his other five tutors the points of order for the order of the dragon and fairy. "There is a coming magic war.

It will be fought by necromancers who seek bringers of grace" Lenora sits in the conference library and holds an exceptional ruby in her hand as she tells them. "We are the bringers of grace. Using our virtuous qualities and magic, we strive to instil peace with truth, integrity, honour, purity and excellence. We lead by example and not decree. We freely give and, in turn, receive. We stand for truth, justice, kindness, empathy and sympathy". Carrelli, the potions teacher, is sitting in her chair wearing an all-black mini-skirt blouse with a black blazer with blue streaked lines as a pattern. Inside her blazer is a whisky bottle with an exceptional nutritional brew.

She takes it out of her inside blazer pocket, opens it and begins to drink. She then says to the guild.

"This supplemental nutritional drink is made from the finest malt, hops and barley. I invented this, not them, but the shadow government got their hands on my recipe.

Now they are extorting my business and turning it into theirs. They are stealing minds, work and ideas.

This drink is my livelihood when I'm not a teacher. We have to do something about that shadow government. If one person is stolen from, everyone is stolen from.

It is the law of the land." Protege asks! "Lenora, you are the vice principal on these affairs. Anything you would like to add.

"Just because we are from the magic society does not mean that our rules and laws should fall behind the standards of civilisation.

The board of ghouls and wizards must be bought to justice. Spencer, is there something you would like to add"?

"We need to get the final pure blood Faye to safety. If the shadow government finds her, it may be over for her and us.

They would have won, and lawlessness would have its day. We must seek the shadow government and incinerate them like the sick blood vampires they are".

Olive responds, "Faye students have learnt potions and are keen on this subject. Still, the battle that lies before us is not potion based.

It is more like physical pursuits".

Jun, the alchemy and practical spells teacher, says, "our new protection against evil forces tutor begins today, and he is the same age as Grace.

We should put her on an apprenticeship course as his permanent apprentice and secretary.

Other students started at fourteen and left at her age.

She must be put in administration and given an adult role". Just then, Grace and Terrence arrive outside the academy.

Terrence shows his identification explains it's his first day then enters with grace. They are soon directed to the basement conference room, where Terrence and grace are briefed.

Terence gets drafted to investigate a secret government society of evil wizards and vampires called the board of ghouls but are commonly known as the shadow government.

Grace partners with him. Protege says to Terrence. "Good morning, Mr Terrence valour, the first vampire lord of the gothic kingdom and part owner of the academy along with your aide, princess fairy grace hope. I got to brief you on a few things today. You have been drafted to be head of security and run physical education classes whilst learning esoteric magic and your natural vampire magic. You will be paid a higher salary and have unlimited access to the academy, so treat this place like your second home. Any questions"?

"No sir, I am ready to work for my grandfather's kingdom". "We need intelligence on who is working for the shadow government. We have an address for them, but we need someone to sneak in and gather intelligence on their actions. Go to each location and plant spyware on them so we can view their every miscreant activity".

"Shall I go with Grace, or should I leave her here"? "From today, grace is your companion and aide. You must take her everywhere with you and keep her safe.

In time she will learn strength and power close to your level and be able to defend herself against evil forces. Go now. The first place you must visit is an old abandoned army base they have been in control of since they had power in the last government.

The next place is an inactive police station; the final place is the local government councillor office buildings". Grace and Terrence leave for the old abandoned army base. Inside the army base is one of three main factions: demons, wizards and vampires. In this case, the army base was overtaken by miscreant vampires whose only interest was to take the lives of the innocent.

On the other hand, Terrence was from a creed of noble vampires, and his great-grandfathers had been engaged in the noble versus miscreant vampire wars for millennia. In the base, the overlord general, starkly a miscreant vampire, oversees the production of blood for miscreant vampires. He goes to a cold locker where they are harvesting the blood, and then he walks towards a chiller where he speaks to a winged lady. "You know what our automation tells us"? Jessica is tied up and surrounded by the dead bodies of Faye people, who seem to have been drained of their blood. "No, I don't know. What is that"? "Our automation technology tells us we need only one millilitre of blood to complete the feeding of our people.

The rise of Desmodus Demon King and the casting spell of eternal power for the wizard's shadow society. For some reason, we have not got that. One more drop of blood and our three factions have won the war against the noble vampires. The fight against the wizards of grace and the war against good werewolves and Faye people, if any pure blood Faye are left. And it has to be a pure-blood, but none of you left.

There is only one, but we can not find her ". "Why are you telling me all this?". "Can you help me find her? " Jessica screams and cries. "No"! Terrence and Grace catch the whole thing on camera whilst using their reserve powers to become invisible. They plant close caption cameras everywhere. On the way out, they discover Jessica alone and take her with them.

Terrence and Grace report their findings to the magic order after rescuing Jessica. Jessica is sent to the academy infirmary, where she is treated for anaemia.

The six leading board members meet to discuss the insurrection of Desmodos Demon King. Colin, the demon governor, and Jose, the demon councillor. Jerry, the 1st paladin, the shadow governments wizard guild, and Mateo, the 2nd paladin. Stana, the grand vampire lord, and Chiltaro, the chief vampire lord, all meet to discuss their next steps at an underground basement tavern in a secret location. The vampire lords make it clear they need only a few more jots of blood from a young fairy who has just received her powers. Colin examines recent reports stating to the vampire lords. "Stana, Chiltaro, you're out. It is highly valued by our mission. Have you completed extracting the pure Faye's blood into the Desmodos chamber"? Chiltaro explains, "we ran into a problem"! "What was that"? "The Faye blood that we required was not enough; indeed, we needed all thirteen Faye princesses, but in the end, we only extracted blood from twelve"! "Was that not enough"? "No, it wasn't the last princess who must be found and brought to us",. Jose asks. "What about the fairy princesses? Where are they now"? "Eleven of them are dead, and the twelfth one is out of fresh blood but is using fairy magic to keep herself alive". Just then, the vampire general walks in and tells them. "My masters, we have just received word that the twelfth fairy princess has escaped from the barracks". Jerry, the wizard paladin, exclaims. "Send out a search party immediately". Mateo remarks, "we need to find the thirteenth princess as well". General Theo says. "sirs can I make a suggestion? "What"! "I suggest we check around the hotels in the area just to look around as an official of the people. They will be none the wiser to us" "Good idea"! The next day arrives. Terrence has his first full day at the academy as a life skills tutor, with Grace as his trainee apprentice. The warlock vampire and pimp that assaulted Grace and Terrence at Terrence's home and restaurant show up in a suave business suit the next day at the academy. Terrence and grace are walking through the grounds when they see his car pull up to them. They turn to each other, and Terrence says, "it is that pimp from three days ago. We must not reveal ourselves to him". Grace replies, "let's hide and follow him". As he gets out of the car and walks towards the grounds, they take up sentient and obscure positions, becoming onlookers of the warlock pimp. The warlock walks around the corridors looking for and observing key people whilst Terrence and Grace follow silently and stealthily behind him. The warlock pimp, posing as a businessman tied to the government, walks up to the academy entrance and enters through the main abbey into the actual building. Each time he walks closer towards the principal's office, Grace and Terrence follow slowly behind him. Without him noticing them, they obscure his vision with Vampire and fairy magic. The warlock pimp, posing as a businessman, walks up to the principal's office and knocks on the door. Protege, the principal, hear's the door knock and answers. "Who's there"? He asks the warlock pimp and proceeds to tell him. "It is Adkin from the government office for business and academic affairs. We have a proposition for your school"! Protege becomes crudely suspicious whilst still anticipating abundance and excites at the prospect of financial growth. "And what's that"? Adkins carrying his briefcase, pulls out a contract and tells him the key points of it. "The government would like your academy to raise capital by becoming more productive. If you sign this today. We will increase your budget, help you open up workshops related to your courses, and increase your overall wages for each of your tutors. Sign this contract, and let me check if there are any structural problems with the academy's building"! The exuberant joy on Protege's face soon fades away as he realises the recent past's problems and how the shadow government loves to behave. Protege's face sinks, and he gets out of his chair, approaching the suspected pimp. "I know who you are. You are from the shadow government. Don't think you can trick me the way you walk in here with your suave suit and your government office. This is all just a ploy to kidnap someone. Will let me tell you something now after all of that. There is no way I am letting you leave"!

Protege calls Terrence on his phone on speed dial. Outside the office, Terrence's phone rings. Terrence picks up. Grace asks. "Who is that"? Terrence replies. "Let me answer it, hold on. Hello"! Down the other side, Protege asks. "Terrence, where are you"? Terrence responds. "I am just outside your office"! Terrence and Grace walk in. Protege tells them. "Apprehend this pimp so we can question him later"! Protege and Terence take the pimp hostage and police him into the lower grounds of the academy basement, where there is a dungeon.

Terrence is told that his family own the academy and that he is a legacy stakeholder at his grandfather's funeral.

After all that, Protege turns to Terence and says. "Terence, there is a reason we chose you to start here today. It is because this is the day of your estranged great-grandfather's funeral. It is being held here on these grounds where he will be buried like the rest of his relatives who had deep involvement in this one thousand-year-old academy. Terrence, you are a legacy stakeholder and are expected to be a true scholar of proficiency. From this day forth, you will be the owner of one-sixth of this estate,". Terrence, with nervous security, says. "I will be happy to enter into the family business". Later that day, all staff and tutors met in the chapel to pray and congregate at the funeral of grandfather Nathan Valour. People weep, cry and beg whilst beholding the catholic cross. After the church service, Terrence and Grace get invited to the obituary reading of the will. The reader says to Terrence.

"Terrence Valour inherits one in six of the academy. Along with this are the academy's finances and the estate shared between him and five others"! Terrence sits in his chair in a surprised and excited state, saying. "Wow, how much is the estate worth"? The testimonies reader continues. "The estate is worth over one hundred million. As the treasurer of the estate, Terrence will have to split the estate up between five of his cousins. They will each be expected to take up a lifetime commitment to the estate and work on the upkeep for the foreseeable future. On his 22nd birthday, he will be fully mature as a Vampire and be expected to take on a full-time role as governor and guardian of the moral virtue of the academy. Any questions Mr Valour"? With great zeal, Terrence says. "Where do I sign"? The testimony reader shows Terrence the dotted lines and signs his name across the contract with great urgency.

Terrence Valour is a soon-to-be vampire lord due to come into his powers on his 22nd birthday. His birthday is only twelve hours away. After midday, during class and before his 22nd birthday, Terence's powers begin to take route. Terrence had initially found it hard to teach a physical magic class due to a lack of experience. Terrence suddenly turns into a bat utilising his full changeling abilities. After physical magic class at around 2pm, Terrence goes on his lunch break to the cafeteria from the education hall on the west wing. Academic students and tutors must walk across the abbey and into the food court building. On the way to the building, Terrence experiences severe heat exhaustion and gets thirsty for water.

When he enters the cafeteria, he is slightly covered in smoke. The waiter says to him. "All Vampires that come into full maturity must drink fizzy drinks. They are what makes vampires accustomed to the rays of sunshine". With a polite smile, Terrence says, "thank you, I will have a litre of those"! The night draws in, and Terrence walks into his 200 sqm suite next to Grace's. They both greet each other at the door as they walk in separately. They both step into the shower, wash, put on their pyjamas, and get in their beds. Terence falls asleep and begins to dream again. This time it is a magic door that opens next to the bed, and instead of leading into Grace's room, it leads into the great hall of Terence's ancestors. There he keeps walking whilst listening to the sweet, serene tone of the sound of the song from a beautiful woman. Soon he stands beside a statue and notices Lenora standing there again. "I will see you in the real world. Today we will meet ``" how"? "I am a corporeal being but take up this form due to vampire magic.

"You're a vampire like me". "I have a few questions about being a vampire". "This is the purpose of our meeting here". "I need to learn more about my powers." "how do I use my powers, and what type of magic can I do"? "There are 8 types of vampire magic. 1. Dark arts are the first magic a vampire must learn. 2. Blood magic. 3. Energy manipulation. 4. Necromancy! 5. Occult magic. 6. Spirit force. 7. Supernatural force and 8 transcendent magic. There are 8 types and eight levels, and their stages are key subjects of such magic. Dark art magic channels magic from the shadow realm. The key ways it is used are through ritual spells, chants, magical symbols and energy shapes, telepathic gestures, and visualisation spells. The final one is changing shapes or shapeshifting. These seven magical arts are the foundation learning signature for vampire magic. Level 2 blood magic and its four main stages are blood curse, astral projection, blood spells and healing the blood. Blood magic can either heal or hinder. Make sure you teach your pupils to only heal with blood magic and effect for the good of the magic force. The third level of vampire magic is energy manipulation, which has 2 to 4 stages. As energy is potential and kinetic, so is magical energy. The two stages are created or absorb magical energy and shape or affect outcomes and situations. The fourth level is necromancy. This has two main subjects plus a special one that is forbidden to unlock. The two which have approval from the magic board are as follows, manipulate the dead or those with ailments and the contacting of long-forgotten spirits. Now I have to tell you this, or you may discover it alone and not know what you are doing. "Well, what is it"? "Death force using spells to control the dead beyond the grave to inevitably affect the living. But I stress this day if you pull a curse spell like this. It is a Wiccan spell, and you will be carried off to the hell fire as an evil wizard, so you must never do it. Teach and tell your pupils from grade to the fourth year at the academy that this is forbidden, accursed and banned by all practices.

The fourth level is occult magic. With only one subject as a stage". "It lasts one academic year to learn every vampire magic principle of mysterious magic. This includes occultism, principles of mysticism, shamanism, esoterics, different magical forces and vampire lore. Sixth is spirit force; its subjects include spirit power from all souls alive in and on the earthly realm. Again this is just one subject that lasts an academic year but has a lot of high-level topics that need to be studied. Such as magical energy generation, tapping into the living soul force and learning the nature of earth realm magic forces. The seventh and penultimate level is the supernatural force. Utilising the soul and spirit pressure with the mind pressure at the highest level, you can begin excavating the supernatural force's beginnings. The final story and eighth wonder of all levels that a vampire must each is transcendent magic. Like mystical magic, it is not of the world alone. It is also of the wider cosmos. This is the final lesson our students will learn from you; this is how you become an award-winning academic tutor at our institution.

After mastering the magic arts, Grace enquires of her sister to protege. Meanwhile, next door Grace begins to dream and appears in the exact same place as Terrence, but instead of staying in the main hall, she is shown to the dojo. She walks over the flower-blossomed pond with tiger lilies and beautiful roses. She walks over the bridge and approaches the main dojo gates, listening to a voice direct her but not actually seeing a face. Lenora then says. "Stop waiting there. Everything I have to say must be taught here. I am your fairy godmother, and I am here to teach you how to be a fairy. A sudden surprise comes on Grace Hope's face, and she asks with surprise. "But aren't you, Lenora, the vice principal of the vampire and Faye academy"? Lenora looks directly at her and, with a tone that was meant as serious, smiles, harking at Grace. "You and I can do wonders as fairies. Please do not be alarmed or talk about the dream in waking reality. It is just fairy vampire magic with the first lesson. The first three lessons essential to every practising Faye are the three substances. The first is enchantment magic; these are counter curses or activating spells. The second is elemental magic.

Elements are powerful evocations that temper the seas, winds, dust, and your energies.

Fairy dust manipulation can enhance the weakest spells. Substance magic is learned in the first year at this academy.

Next and in the second year is placement magic. The three types of placement magic are fairy arrow, fairy fort and fairy ring. The first fairy arrow is about proficiency and craft, and the next two fairy fort and fairy ring are based on your creativity as an artisan who crafts magic.

Build your energy into a fortress of healing, or build your power into a circle of protection that no force of malevolence can cross.

This second level of fairy magic helps develop craft, creation and proficiency.

The next level of fairy magic is the third year and fourth level of fairy magic.

They deal in healing, illusionary and energy-based magics.

The fourth year and fourth level of fairy magic involve mana manipulation, telekinesis magic, and nature empowerment. In the fourth year, all teachings relate to the foundation principle of fairy magic. The founding code of fairy magic is natural energy. Natural energy is broken down into three key concepts, genuine, empowerment, and magic. These three concepts, when combined, create internal magical energy, which in time produces external magical power leading to seasonal magic. The genuine spell leads to the telekinesis empowerment of nature, increasing magic energy, and the residual magical power becomes mana manipulation.

Level five and six subjects include higher natural magic energy. The key topics are seasonal magic, autumn, winter, and spring. Space astral projections and teleportation. The third topic is sleep magic and dream magic. These topics and subjects are usually studied over three years in tandem with each other.

The final stage of fairy magic involves only two subjects. Still, it is harder to learn and even more challenging to master. They include transcendent magic and wish granting. I expect you to know all this as a full-blood princess in triple the time only three years under a vampire artisan as his apprentice.

Terry wakes up from the dream, and it is 5:45 am. He gets a text message on his mobile phone. "Come and join us in the teacher's lounge on the ground floor by the reception.

Lenora shows Terrence, and grace around the academy, explaining that she is his great-aunt. The academy has seventeen main areas for pupils, not including staff rooms. The first stop is the potions zone. In this zone are eight rooms dedicated to cooking potions, two classrooms, two lecture halls, two laboratories and two arena rooms. Students practise throwing brews and changing spells from potions into elements in these arena rooms. Chief potions tutor Carrelli is working on her successive academic triumph in the potions laboratory. "Grace, Terrence, this is the chief potions teacher. I expect you two to undergo intensive training for your first six months. Ask her what she is working on"! "Hello, Carrelli. What are you working on"? Carrelli explains. "Since my last batch of healthy fizzy pop got stolen by the shadow government, I have had to step up my game. I am working on a fizzy drink that increases brain power and intelligence for 24 hours. Normal humans increase their mental capacity, but to magic folk, it makes us more invincible in our intellect. Just a little bit more tweaking, and it will be ready for the main market,". Lenora exclaims. "Make sure the shadow government does not get it again"! Carrelli retorts. "It should all be fine. I have my IP application on the cloud sent off, and I await a response. I should be fully accredited, vetted and own all copyrights by the end of the week,". Lenora tells them. "That was the potions zone next. We go to the spells and enchantment zones. Be careful when we get there. Things aren't always as they seem".

Lenora shows the two apprentice tutors around the spells and enchantment zone. Much like before, there are two classrooms, two lecture halls, two arenas and, this time, two conference domes. In the leading lecture hall, olive, the chief spells and enchantments teacher, olive, a Faye tutor, is showing her classroom a mind enchantment spell. Lenora introduces Terrence and Grace to Olive. "Grace, Terrence, this is Olive, the chief spells and enchantment teacher. Ask her what she is doing"! Grace asks. "I am the new apprentice tutor, Grace, and this is Terrence. We want to know what you are teaching the class this morning"? Olive answers by teaching the class. "Right, class, I am teaching you the mind enchantment spell.

The mind enchantment spell must only be performed against a monster or a ghoul in a desperate situation. The mind enchantment spell is a curse and requires you to lose good magic points instead of gaining them. If you do this spell too much, it could make you a Wiccan and tend to the dark side of magic when performed on an innocent. Only do this spell at desperate times and against a monster, a ghoul or an evil wizard. Ready! Here is how you perform the mind enchantment spell"! Olive shows her students and the tutors the formation of the mind enchantment spell. Then Lenora guides Grace and Terrance to the next zone, the botany gardens. The botany garden is a half-large garden of herbs, spices, fruits and vegetables. It is where tutors such as Carrelli used to derive their following food products for the markets. In the botany garden, food, water and vegetation are produced to feed, hydrate and teach students about pills, potions and spells.

The next zone is the academic library. In the academic library, most merrital achievers. Usually, these achievers are halfway between a clever novice and an advanced expert. Either way, they merit themselves in aiming for their next achievement. In academics, the library is an abundance of logic-based encyclopaedias, games and apparatus, all linked to teaching. For instance, from the maths side of academia, in the maths section is a computer-sized calculator which helps teach the logic of mathematics.

Another example in the technology area is the industrial makings of technology, from the wheel to the first engine-powered car to a modern aeroplane engine deconstructed and indicative of gameplay skills training. The academic library has multiple sections. The first four are science, English, maths and technology. The nine after that are agriculture, financial and services, healthcare, sociology and theology, construction, retail, multimedia, hospitality and manufacturing and production industry. The last sectors were business, charity and government.

The next zone that Lenora took Terrence and grace to was the study library. In the study library where the professional students had more than merit to their work. These students were proficient in their studies and knew precisely what they were doing. The study library consisted of chairs, desks, computers, reference books and journals, with the most professional students taking notes.

The next zone they went to was the book library. The book library was vast and wide, with ten-foot cabinets and various genres, topics and subjects. And this trend went on for meters all through the book library. In this library were the most distinguished students studying for proficiency and progression in their chosen field. This zone was the quietest and most refreshing place. For all eager students, the book library was a mecha to be found and an earthly paradise filled with a wondrous array of inspirational, factual and edifying textbooks.

They then come to the computer and virtual reality hall. This is in the technology zone of the academy. In this zone, academic students use fun and games to learn the stages and levels of their chosen topics and subjects. Lenora turns to them and says.

"Now, what I am about to show you is more splendid than anything I have shown you, and it must be kept a complete secret. No one outside this academy has ever stepped foot into this remote area except you until now"! Grace asks. "What could possibly be this important you keep it a secret"? Terrence retorts. "An age-old academy as deep and altruistic as this will keep secrets, and I think I know why",.

Lenora explains, "Terrence is right. This academy is also a sanctuary for oppressed and martyr-like magical beings,".

Terrence butts in. "basically, what she's saying is most of the students here have parents who were victimised by an oppressor". "Again, perfect understanding is being iterated by Terrence. Follow me through this secret passageway. This building we are leading into is a theology temple for magic beings, and only our most highly regarded students can stay here. We regarded our students so highly that we made this hidden building a monastery temple dedicated to gothic catholicism and academia study". The three magical beings continue walking through the secret tunnel until they reach the monastery building.

They exit the tunnel entering luxury, a stained glass 20-foot ceiling and cream marble walls.

The monastery dormitory is an extended building connected to the central academy via the walkway.

This dormitory is the home of 100 monastery students. On each of the 8 levels of the monastery are 13 specially trained students belonging to four main pillars of study. The first pillar of study goes to the two levels of sanctity. The second is exorcism, the third is meditation, and the final is prayer. These four pillars of study reflect absolution, dedication and discipline to learning the magic arts through religion, virtue and selfless acts of goodness and mercy.

Catering zone, including a catering kitchen and hall, chiller, store cupboard, pantry, utilities and appliances. The catering hall is a luxurious marble decorated in gold and cream. The kitchen is spacious and professional, so it could fit over 100 cooks. There are 50 cookers and over 100 pans. This leads to the catering hall that can accommodate up to 1000 people at a given time. The catering hall has ten rows of tables accommodating 50 people on each side.

Study hall, The catering hall leads onto the study hall. The catering hall can accommodate up to one thousand people.

The society of ghouls and the guild of wizards meet. They make plans to find the last great Faye sister. Colin, the demon governor and highest ranking official of the corrupt shadow government overlooking the two branch companies of evil, the society of ghouls and the wizards guild, tells the five highest leaders of the society of ghouls. "Jessica, the penultimate Faye sister, has been lost in one of our most secure locations. Why is this"? Jose, the demon councillor, interrupts, saying to Chiltaro, the grand vampire lord. "Chiltaro is that not your base with your legions. What happened to you there"? Chiltaro, the chief vampire lord of the vampire broods. The least of the vampire races in credence and stewardship as they are too carnal and warlike compared to other vampire creeds. "We were getting a new security system installed after the other one needed updates. We are sorry. We have Faye's blood. All we need now is the final pure-blood Faye princess to bring our nightmare world to reality,".

Jeremy, the 1st paladin of the wizards guild, tells the society of ghouls. "My wizards at the artisan laboratories have been running tracer spells to find the remaining

Faye princess. Currently, we have only one more block to lift. Once the block has been lifted, we can apprehend her. We already sent our main warlock to patrol all magic signatures in the area, and when he has completed his study, we will have found her,". Colin asks.

"So, how long is this going to take"? Jerry responds. "By the end of the day"! Now the wizards guild began with a good wizard and good magic. Still, a bitter wizard named jerry, the present leader of the wizards guild, gave the excellent wizard Fenius Toan. Was a learned mage who sought to learn the magical arts, from elements to astronomy. He began the current wizard guild 1000 years ago.

100 year ago, his then apprentice Jerry tone poisoned his master and, with grand corruption, began the guild on a path of wickedness and corruption, crime rackets, cruel enchantments and many other un-noble crimes. Mateo, who is Jerry's apprentice, says. "I will get the searchers at the guild on the phone to see if they have found the girl"!

To immerse Desmodos in the living world, they must get one more litre of blood from a princess. Who is a noble pureblood royal Faye. by doing this, they will unleash the nightmare beast Desmodos also known as the demon of avarice and lust. Mateo gets a call from the warlock pimp, which gives them a message. "I think I have located the girl through the tracking spells. The scribes have each landed on the location of the etiquette academy for Vampires and Faye". Mateo responds in a calm yet begrudging tone. "We suspected they would be at that academy. Assemble a team of our best four mercenaries and bring a security detail.

We are going to take them by force. And with magic".

The shadow board of governors get news of Grace Hope's location. They send a lycanthrope, a wizard and a witch with a ghoul to apprehend her at the headquarters. The lycanthrope is named Thomas, the wizard is named Corey, the witch is named Tabitha, and the ghoul is named Dara. All meet to discuss with the warlock how they will overcome the academy. Corey Grey says to the team of evildoers.

"We need to go in inconspicuously and leave inconspicuously.

With the Faye princess". Thomas enters the plot telling them. "Show me a picture of the princess and get her scent so I can sniff her out",. Tabitha tells them, "I will cast a spell to make them more susceptible and naive to our presents. They will suspect that we are just a group of academy trustees. This will give us the advantage,". The ghoul Dara explains with a feverish tone of mirth. "That is nothing. I will hypnotise them with my hypnotic gaze into leading the Faye princess to us". Thomas then says if we do all of this, there is no chance the Princess will escape us.

Terrence meets with the six legacy owners of the academy. They are a witch, a wizard, a Vampyre, Faye and two Vampyres, a Faye and a Lycan. The Vampire and the Faye are both of loose relation to Terrence, and grace, as royal lineage. Grace soon learns that she has a similar legacy to Terrence in that she is more likely to require an ownership stake in the royal academy of magic. Protege, the other cross breed Faye Vampyre, takes Grace down the corridors into a secret wealth cabinet room. He tells her Terrence is her fourth cousin, and both enjoy royal privilege as academy owners. He also tells her they are the last remaining pure-blood Vampyre and pureblood Faye. They enter the wealth cabinet room and come to a giant golden round table in the shape and design or markings of a compass. "The etiquette academy for Vampire and Faye has a special portal to the magical worlds where the six founders abide". A surprised Grace exhumes. "The founders, but isn't this school thousands of years old"?

Protege waves his wand over the golden round table with compass markings. A golden magic glow begins to erupt over the table as a magical window seems to appear. Six different golden glows in the shape of windows start to erupt from one pattern until they have made a circle of six, with the seventh being at the central point of the table. In the six compass points, we see six images. One of the grand Witch Petulia in her castle chamber. The second chief vampire is the pure-blood Cedrick Valour in his castle war room. The third Lord vampire of the clean incubus clan of vampires is at his dining table. The fourth of Queen Zita the Faye Princess. In her kitchen, cooking up potions. The fifth one of lord Delroy Delaware the lycanthrope steward, in his garage adjacent to his castle home. The sixth one was of a princely sleeping wizard in a protected case. Surrounded by spell papers and mantras charts. A curious Terrence with a hint of nervous energy suddenly hopes up saying. "Who was that elderly man on the bed with a crystal dome protecting him"? From out of the shadows walks Lenora, and she says. "That is Fenius Ravenheart, one of the greatest wizards to have ever lived. I will tell you more about him soon, but my stories will confuse you. He is a good wizard".

4

WHAT'S THE TRUTH

Five members of the shadow government arrive with fake identification claiming they are from the society of magic. The warlock approaches the receptionist and says. "We are here from the society of magic. These are our identification cards. The receptionist responds. "Are these authentic? Let me just check with our digital verification system". Just as she is about to scan the cards, she is hypnotised by the ghoul. And to ensure that she does not do a countercurse. The wizard casts a spell on the hypnotisms with an enchantment incantation. Everyone except them in range of the hypnosis is put under the spell. The wizard says. "Enhance the vision of all on sight". Waving his wand and then his finger. The hooded Wiccan, a witch who is one of the most powerful witches in the magical world, and evil whispers. "All in this building worship us as main board members of the society of magic". The hooded Wiccan then turns to the receptionist in an unpleasant and cruel tone saying to her. "Get the remaining pure-blood Faye princess to attend us so she can be appraised".

The receptionist calls Grace Hope, the person they are looking for. People walk past the team of the so-called society of magic board members. Every time they get close, they are entranced and turned away by one of the magic evil-doers. Soon everyone needs to remember what they are doing and ends up in a field of paralysis from being so forgetful. The end result is that everyone stands still like statues with no movement. Just an eerie gaze.

The reception desk is asked to contact Grace. The hooded Wiccan says. "Call the Faye sister immediately. That is an order". The receptionist walks towards the intercom and then calls to the basement through the speakers. "Would Grace hope please report to the reception for an evaluation from the society of magics main board members"? She repeats the previous words. Then sits at her desk and freezes. She sits absolutely still in paralysis from the accursed hypnotism. In the basement, Protege, Lenora, Terrence and Grace find that the society of magic is already preoccupied with their respective homes attending to duties. They visualise the actual society of magic seen on the plinth's magical scanner. The only reason the four mages have not been accursed by the hypnotism is that they have seen the truth beyond any lies and lost the power of the spell. Lenora says, "something must be wrong"".

Protege agrees, "I think you are right". Terrence implies, "I don't think they're going to be who they say". Grace asks, "What should we do"? Lenora tells them. "We quietly investigate the goings on on the upper levels but beware.

They will have the advantage as they have found our base of function. This, in turn, could become a curry of their choosing".

The evil ghoul, wizard and witch who works for the shadow government and his boss, the chief general wizard. Has cast a spell and placed a hypnotic trance on the academy to kidnap grace. The witch tells them. "Everyone under our spell first becomes swayed by our command and then paralysed with intention.

If my spells work well enough by the time of their arrival, they will be in total paralysis,". The warlock asks. "What about a backup spell? Just in case they have broken out"? The wizard says. "Then we will simply take control of their minds with a more powerful spell". The only people alert to the spell and have independent consciousness are Grace, Protege, Lenora and Terrence.

Lenora tells them. "We need to wear invisibility hats. Over there in the basement store cupboard is a treasure trove of magical trinkets and ornaments created by academics at this academy. Protege, please retrieve the four magic hats and charm them with the power of invisibility"!

Protege goes further down the stairs into a store cupboard with many magical trinkets, clothes, ornaments and items. He comes to the hat section and takes up four magical hats. He then uses his magic wand to charm the hats. "Excelsis reserve"! The hats begin to have a hazy white glow, then disappear and reappear before settling into a corporeal state. He then returns to the upper basement. They each put on their respective hats and leave the meeting chamber.

They leave the basement wearing invisibility hats. The invisibility hats serve a particular function. They rest on your third eye and cover your head. Doing this type of covering with a magical garment usually means that any magic in search of you does not make eye contact or have a reading of the intended mind. Eyes are the windows to the soul, and your mind is your connection to higher powers. Will therefore lack the ability to connect with your metaphysical spirit. And the meta is the border between the physical and the spiritual.

They come up through the elevator from the basement and arrive on the ground level.

The team of four investigates. When walking through the corridors, they realise students are under a spell. Lenora says. "Stop walking for a minute. I will use my Astro inspection to see what has happened here"! Lenora rubs her temples together, focusing her eyes on the corridor. She then tracks and traces anything that occurred over the past morning. Lenora soon arrives at the event where the school is under a hypnotic spell. She tells them. "Five evil mages claiming to be from the society of magic hypnotised and put an attack on the school. We are immune to it because when the spell was cast, we were already observing the actual society of magic.

In all its heavenly glory". Suddenly, they are stopped by the hooded Wiccan, who asks. "Why are you not under our spell"? Lenora stops and, with a look of surprise, also asks. "How can you see us in our magic hats"? The hooded Wiccan then proceeds to cast a spell after saying. "If you are wearing magic hats, but I can not see them. Whilst our spells have no power over you. That can only mean one thing. Our magic has cancelled each other,". Lenora then proclaims. "Next one to cast magic is the winner of this battle of incantations. Fairy magic rejects all evil magic". The hooded Wiccan invokes a tetraseal spell. A tetraseal is a binding spell that trains itself to control and eventually subdue the opponent or victim into submission. A round glowing disc of energy begins to break through the wall of glowing energy surrounding the four mages. But before they can do anything about it, the powerful magic of the hooded Wiccan overcomes them. Grace Hope is put in an endless brain training game that encourages her to give up on herself and submit to a cruel fate. Lenora tells the team. A ghoul and a wizard battle Protege, while Terrence Valour fights a warlock and a lycanthrope as a Vampire. They fight! Before grace is wholly engrossed with the spell, she calls out desperately to Lenora. "Why were you not prepared for her spell"! With a compassionate tone, Lenora tells her, "I did not know she was a transcendent like me. Know this gets serious". Grace Hope resists the spell every step of the way. Lenora helps her and communicates with her every step of the way. Lenora and The Hooded Wiccan get locked into a transcendent battle for the safety of Grace Hope, the last remaining pure-blood princesses present wellbeing. "Okay, you have bested me so far, but can you take transcendent elemental magic at its best"? The hooded Wiccan summons her sceptre, which magically appears then she chants. "Wind, water, rain and shine give me the power of the divine". A glow engulfs the scene, and the hooded Wiccan and Grace disappear from the academy's vision. Lenora then chants. "Elements of the north, south, east and west. Show me where my visual field rests". Just then, Lenora disappears to the dark realm where the hooded Wiccan has taken Grace.

This realm appears the same as the academy, except everything is back to front, out of order and tainted to the shadow.

Lenora hides behind a wall. Then just as the Hooded Wiccan goes for a disappearing spell, Lenora screams, citing an incantation. "Freeze"! The hooded Wiccan and grace are frozen still. Lenora walks towards the two who are beside the reception. As she is about to disappear, the hooded Wiccan begins to move again and soon is fully animated. They have a zapping match whilst levitating the Faye Princess Grace Hope out of the way to safety every time magical energy zaps from their wands. In the end, Lenora successfully manages to sneak Grace out of the dark realm and into the natural realm. She says to her wand, "freeze with the chains of the dark realm". The hooded Wiccan is soon exhausted of her powers and temporarily chained. "You see, hooded Wiccan the Great Faye Lenora is twice transcendent. A definite match for you". The hooded Wiccan rolls her eyes whilst Lenora and Grace make their way back to the natural realm. Meanwhile, back at the academy.

Terrence uses his full fledgling vampire powers to overcome and defeat the demonic forces at the academy. He battles the warlock and ghoul simultaneously. They start with martial arts and self-defence, which soon grows into magical combat. The Warlock throws a punch made out of magical curse energy. To escape it, Terrence turns into a bat and flies at the warlock biting him and draining his blood. By doing this, he generates the energy of his previous power. When he refutes back to his standard size, he throws the cursed energy ball back at the warlock with its twice-powerful nature. The warlock finds it nearly impossible to dodge. It hits him, and he explodes. Terrence then turns to the ghoul, who gets scared and runs away. Terrence lets him escape.

Finally, Protege battles against the wizard. The wizard turns to Protege and says. "Finally, we meet in battle. My name is Trench, the magician of tricks". Lenora shouts, "once you have defeated him, I will send him through a portal to the dark realm". Protege then turns to him and says. "I am a protege, a transcendent magician of high standing is unlikely you will defeat me". The two then make their wands magically appear. They begin to duel. "You know what I don't like about rogue wizards". "What's that"? "The sudden death curse"! The two wizards begin running backwards and forwards, constantly blasting and dodging the energy burst from each other's wands until finally, Protege is victorious. A team of officers from the society of magic arrive and detain the five magic folks.

Taken into custody are the warlock and his goons. The goons are questioned by a high-ranking exorcism specialist and a transcendent wizard, Jamesson, who also teaches for the magic society. Every now and then, he is on call for specialist academic learning topics, in this case, the exorcism of demons. The society of magic is a wide-walled two-acre castle with 18 stories of floor levels. They are in a special power-dampening room that appears as an old sophisticated cave. The furnishings are simple yet stern and imply correction and discipline. Jamesson proceeds to ask the warlock. "What were you doing at the academy? And don't try to lie to me. I put a truth spell on you"? The warlock tells him against his will. "I was there on a mission for the shadow government". "What did the shadow government want at the school"? "To extract the blood of the final pure blood Faye princess. To resurrect the demon of Avarice Desmodos into the natural realm". "Interview over, we got a confession. Any more, and the shadow government might intervene. We need to give Terrence Valour a commendation for excellence. Make sure you put it on his record.

Terence and Grace are invited to the witch's coven castle to discuss their new advantage against the shadow government from the monitor in the basement by the high priestess Faye Queen Zita. "You four legends have been invited to the society of magic to discuss developments. We are delighted with what you have achieved in our ongoing war against the shadow government. Well done, you have all been commended.

THE END

Printed in the United States
by Baker & Taylor Publisher Services